WISH

Other books by the author

Learning Not To Touch (Redbeck Press, 1998)
Reaching for a Stranger (Shoestring Press,1999)
Outstripping Gravity (Redbeck Press, 2000)
Exposures (Redbeck Press, 2003)
Taking Cover (Redbeck Press, 2005)
No Time for Roses (Salzburg Press, 2009)

Snowbell, often called Soldanella, who has to push aside half-melted ice, makes a kind, mild-mannered companion if you listen to the lilt of her violet-tassled petals.

WISH

A tale in verse by MICHAEL TOLKIEN

◆

(After The Rose-Coloured Wish (1923), a prose fantasy by Florence Bone)

AuthorHouse™ UK Ltd.
500 Avebury Boulevard
Central Milton Keynes, MK9 2BE
www.authorhouse.co.uk
Phone: 08001974150

©2010 Michael G. R. Tolkien. All rights reserved.

No part of this book may be reproduced, stored in a retrieval system, or transmitted by any means without the written permission of the author.

First published by AuthorHouse   6/22/2010

ISBN: 978-1-4490-9652-6 (sc)

This book is printed on acid-free paper.

CONTENTS

First Part **_Under Threat_**

I	Valleys	3
II	Birth And Dreams	7
III	Ignoring Flowers	11
IV	Snowbell & Edelweiss	15
V	Think Red	23
VI	Clipetty Clopitty	29

Second Part **_In Shadow_**

VII	Fængler Surprised	37
VIII	Deeper & Darker	45
IX	Dead Wood	51
X	Fængler's Lantern	57
XI	The Master's Power	63

Thrid Part **_Rally_**

XII	Adam's Search	71
XIII	Well-Wisher	77
XIV	Gentian	83
XV	Bright Beetle	89
XVI	Fængler	95
XVII	Alpenrose	101
XVIII	Necklace	109

-◆-

ADDITIONAL COLOURED PLATES

Soldanella	iv
Edelweiss	21
First glimpse of Fængler	43
Chalet in rose-coloured light	116

ACKNOWLEDGEMENTS

The author and illustrator would like to thank the following:

Max Hamilton for his support and encouragement at every stage of the work's development.
Dorothy Jewitt for a generous supply of details from her researches into the life and work of Florence Bone.
Sheila Woodruff for assistance with the legal aspects of work based on a previously published book.
Darin Jewell (*The Inspira Group Literary Agency*) for his expertise and invaluable guidance over publishing arrangements.
Gerald Dickens for his kind cooperation, advice and suggestions in making a professionally prepared and adapted audio version of this tale.
Cancer research UK and *Methodist Homes for the Aged* (chief beneficiaries of Florence Bone's literary estate) for their kind permission to allow publication to proceed.
Think Digital Print Ltd (Oakham) for their advice and production of initial copy.

PREFACE

The source and inspiration for this narrative poem is a prose fantasy intended for children: *The Rose-Coloured Wish*, by Florence Bone (1875-1971), illustrated by Kate Holmes and published by Hutchinson in 1923. My mother's copy was part of a collection of my parents' books read to us in young childhood in the late 1940s and early 1950s. I inherited the well-used, battered book and twenty years later my own children asked for repeated readings from it. I later realised that this apparently conventional fairy story combines adventure, humour, and moving character conflicts within a gently imposed moral structure, which feels both inevitable and surprising. Thirty years on a series of holidays in alpine venues reminiscent of the book's setting may have prompted me to pay tribute to its story and qualities. Not critically or by re-publication, but creatively, though for several years I had no idea how.

First I became curious about the book's present status and could find no second-hand copies advertised, and no comments on this particular work. But it became apparent from the many other works of Florence Bone, mostly pre-1939-45 War, available through internet sources and cited in British Library records, that she wrote a wide variety of children's fiction, including historical novels, and was a biographer and writer of well-researched documentaries. And yet she is not mentioned in authoritative reference books and critical essays on 20th century children's literature. Whether or not there's irrefutable wisdom in such eclipses, I am not trying to reinstate a lost author but to bring to life the substance of one forgotten story.

In hindsight I realise I have tried to do so by methods similar to those used by earlier, less literal, translators of ancient or mediaeval literature: to recreate the spirit of the original in new dress. I have retained the narrative structure and the essence of the characters along with their conflicts and developments. These are an intimate part of the moral framework with which I identify and to which I have been faithful. However, nearly all the names of characters and places are my own; the dialogue and descriptions have parallels in the source but seldom repeat it verbatim. Not change for its own sake but because, in line with the intention of expressing 'inspiration', I have been true to my own style and allowed my imagination to respond to and in some cases to expand on the original. I trust this makes for interior consistency, avoiding apparent dependence on a source or a sense of being second-hand or patched-up.

Some readers may wonder about the choice of verse as a story-telling medium and question whether it works or has any advantages. There are some simple, practical reasons. Verse has long been my chief discipline and mode of expression and through it I felt more confident about creating a relatively sharp, economical and fast-moving dialogue and narrative. It would also help me to emphasise changes of pace and intense feeling, and to slacken tension where humour or mundane comments prevail.

So after a lot of experimenting, I found a compromise between formality and 'common' rhythms of speech and story-telling, and I hope the main body of the tale is in a verse form sufficiently unobtrusive and 'unmannered' for readers either to be unaware of it or to feel its strategies working positively.

In contrast to this plain style, and often highlighted by particular fonts, I have used distinct kinds of verse to characterise the more ethereal figures, such as the robin, and various flowers and insects that communicate with the children. Generally, persons and creatures who have commerce with humans of all ages speak at a 'normal' pace in the common verse framework. Such distinctions are not derived from my source, nor are the verse prefaces to each chapter. These are in a deliberately formal, alliterating and authoritative style. Some might call it 'stilted'! They are meant to feel like fragments of an older, historically-angled narrative poem, placing some of the persons, places and events into a broader perspective, of which the chief characters are only dimly aware. I wanted to suggest a commonly held belief that all tales, however well-known and 'established' or apparently fantastic, are limited interpretations of a series of events in human history. Florence Bone herself reminded me of this and inspired me to elaborate on it. She includes a background story to throw new light on the life and attitudes of the tale's villain. This is equivalent to chapter XVI in my version where the narrative style is slightly more formal to suggest it is an old tale retold. The response of the man who listens to this episode within the central tale also marks a decisive and quite unexpected turning point in attitudes and developments as the main story comes to a close.

    The illustrations provided by my wife, Rosemary, derive from her independent response to reading my version, which she has been the first to see and judge at every stage. Her work might be regarded as yet another layer of interpretations of the underlying story, since she has chosen freely which aspects of it to represent. She had not read Florence Bone's original story until after my work was finished. This was to avoid making comparisons as part of her reaction to my narrative techniques. For obvious reasons she also preferred not to look at and assess Kate Holmes' charming but, to modern eyes, perhaps rather conventional 'fairy-tale' coloured plates, until after her own work was complete.

Michael Tolkien

15th August, 2007

For our grandchildren

Kallum, Katie, Emma, Lily, Thai, Hannah, Bethany

First Part

Under Threat

I

VALLEYS

Strange tales have been told in lands of tall peaks,
their beings larger than life, bravely holding terrors at bay,
but this one has more to say about the human heart
and how tenderness triumphed over guile and torment.
A story of two deep valleys, one dark with dying pine and spruce,
battening in a bitter outcast and his bewitched crew,
the other where spirits of field and forest still favoured humankind,
alive with streams, lowing cattle, laughter of children,
music of axe and saw in making goods and managing woods..

-◆-

Here Adam the forester earned his keep
and accounted to no one for his care of trees,
wayward goats and wandering cows whose bells
clanged high and low *Belong! I belong to you!*
He was like a pine at the peak of its strength, heard
and saw what many missed in their noise and hurry
through forest glades, either by moonlight
when the Guardians and Wardens danced, or in bright
sun when they took the guise of what they cared for.

Adam worked hard to build his own wood house
and win the love of a girl in the village below
who had made a childhood promise to be his bride.
And one spring day he brought Maria home
to their tall-roofed chalet in her long dress
embroidered with flowers of every season.
Flocks of valley farms rang their bells, and gentians
blessed the bride with their first blue. Well-
wishing and rejoicing rustled through the forest.

But even this wedding day was haunted by a shadow.
Beyond a high pass lurked Fængler. No one
knew how his malice began, why each day
his countless years gave him less joy,
or what powers he had over the soured spirits
imprisoned in his steep-sided dell. The sun
shunned it and the kindly alpenrose died out.
His bent body grew more shrivelled and his clothes
more threadbare. No taller than a small
pony, he hid his misery behind the beard
that hung below his knees, a frosty thorn bush
he shook in threatening rage. At the moon's
dark he set out in boots that muffled and trebled
his stride over pathless ways to prowl round
farms and steal young cattle from their stalls.
He left his prints on moss and sandy fords.
Delicate flowers drooped and withered where he'd passed.

Though they hated and feared the haunter
for stealing goats and cows he did not need,
people envied his precious weapon, an ancient
silver chain of nine wonder-working stones.
Long-dead silversmiths took a hundred years
to make sure its wearer might realise every wish.
However it came his way, Fængler wore it day
and night. Out of spite he could spread disease,
make storms crush cattle under falling trees.
Or so everyone believed, and blamed him
for any misfortune that struck their lives.
No wonder there was a long-held hope
weak as it seemed to be, that someone strong
and cunning would be born to them, surprise
the evil coward and his miserable sentries,
seize that silver necklace and so remove all
power to do them harm. Every parent
dreamed of bringing a saviour to the valley.

II

BIRTH AND DREAMS

*After a day's cutting and shaping Adam crafted every comfort
for the homely log house with its blazing hearth
that warmed their one wide room, filled with all they wanted
when long winter snows lay heavy and locked them in.
Time to carve and construct a cradle for their firstborn
engraved with gentian and edelweiss finely etched.
The child grew in the womb and gallivanted like a spring goat!
A strong son, dreamed Adam. The one who'd deal out doom
to Fængler, filch the chain and set the valleys free.*

While her husband talked about his hopes Maria
sat thoughtfully at her spinning. And a cold
shiver ran down her spine. 'What use
is the selfish wishing power of a necklace?
Look at Fængler and his miserable band.
Those stones weigh on him like a granite yoke.'
'But you learn to wish only the best wishes,'
said Adam. 'Our son might bless all the valleys.'
'Too difficult', sighed Maria as her fingers
spun finest thread to clothe the child of their love.
'One mistake in a wish and there's no return.'
And she was wiser than she knew. No wish
goes unheard in alpine valleys thick with woods
and overlooked by echoing, treacherous rocks.
Tucked in tight and dreaming under months of snow
everything that grows, moves or flies recalls
the old tongue it once shared with all mankind.
One faint wish shakes them like a summons.

Through the wide chalet window Maria seemed
to see glossy oaks and alders shed their leaves
all at once, pines turn their sheen to feathery black.
Then a low sunbeam set alight a clump
of alpenrose: blazing smiles that told her
however blighted and anxious the days ahead
there would be light and hope. And though winter
set in early and hard their son was born
like a gift given to each other at the year's
darkest time. Wrapped in blankets his mother
had woven and warmed by a well-laid fire
he filled the newly–carved cradle with hungry cries.
'Our hero!' laughed Adam who'd long forgotten
his wife's wise words. 'How I'd like to
drape the lucky chain around his little neck.
If I gave it to the one we love, wishing
the best of wishes, how could he fail to be
happy and bring good fortune to our farms?'

Maria snatched up the baby and held him tight.
'He has my wishes without a magic string of stones.
I'll sing to him in the old, unhurried tongue.
Your eyes are as blue as gentian flowers,
Your cheeks pinker than Alpen Rose.
I will hold you to my heart in love
Until you grow into a man whose love
Will be giving, who'll learn to wait and see.
May your best thoughts make you truly free.'
Such selfless wishing stirred kindly
laughter among the spirits of the forest
who had made sure he was named Berwald.

A year later Clara filled the cradle to bless
the festival of light, golden-haired, eyes
the blue of hair bells, her happy cries
like water running over smooth stones.
Adam wished harder than ever to quell the curse
of Fængler and bring home the lucky necklace.

III

IGNORING FLOWERS

Ten winters passed. Snow once more gave way to summer
and the restless children ran out to greet returning gentians.
Were they happy to dance away days in their own dear valley
Or did they long to leap over familiar heights and learn
how it was for others in the wide world beyond?
Berwald could not wait to be a strong, brave man,
chop down pines, build the best chalet, wrench the chain
of wonder-working stones from the wily hermit's neck,
rob that felon of father's herds and return them to their fold.

'You're not the only one who's overheard
mother and father,' said Clara to her brother
who shouted 'Let's go before we're missed.
By nightfall we'll be back with our wishing chain.'
They forded Mittlebach, deepest stream that divided
the meadows, climbed slopes they'd only seen from home.
'What shall we wish?' Clara asked Berwald.
He longed to wield an axe and the power of riches.
Clara was not so eager to grow up.
She'd be too tall to hear and answer all
the small growing, crawling things she loved.
'I would like to find father's cows and goats
but I am not sure about taking the magic chain.'
Berwald strode ahead. He'd do both and soon.
Gentle laughter mingled with the bubbling stream
they scrambled beside and mistook for its music.
More with high hopes climbing into the unknown.
She might listen. The boy's losing touch with us.

Words from kindly spirits of Gentian and Forget-me-not.
Berwald hopes to become a man in a day.
His first wish when he's got the necklace.
Why not sing them a warning song
while they rest and gather strawberries?
He wouldn't listen to those who know.
Other boys have passed here and returned
no older or wiser. Berwald still knew some
flower speech, and dragged his sister away.

And the setting sun stained the mountain peaks.
Rocky slopes below were already in shadow
making the pines look black and thoughtful. Not like
seeing dusk from a window with mother and firelight
behind them, thought Clara. 'Aren't trees powerful
and proud!' She said. 'It makes me feel everything
stands for something else, which means magic is true.
I hope I won't lose touch with the flower talk.'
Berwald was more concerned with how weak

his legs began to feel as they left the last
pines behind and tramped over hard-packed
snow, now rosy-purple in the sun's last rays.
Pin-pricks of light winked far below: one
must be the glow from their own fireside.
Mother would be soothing baby in its cradle,
father returning from his long day in the forest.
Why weren't they there to sit down and eat?
Strawberries don't last. They longed for bread and cheese.

'Fængler's hideout can't be far away.'
Clara tried to cheer Berwald who felt less brave
than when he scorned the flowers in broad daylight.
'What's that?!' Both held their breath as they heard
a long, hollow howl echo over frozen rocks, followed
by a deep baying. 'Wolves!' said Berwald , trying to
sound matter-of fact. Clara shuddered and recalled
tales about wars of wolves and men, amusing
when father's axe and gun hung on the chalet wall.

Her brother felt it was time he took the lead.
'Let's get out of this snow and down the other side.
I'm sticking to what we've decided to do.'
Clara squeezed his hand, glad of his courage.
As they slithered down the far side, Berwald
shaded his eyes from the moon which wouldn't
mind its own business and distracted him
from looking for a safe, sheltered hollow.
Suddenly he plunged below a clump of alpenrose.
'Jump down, Clara. Here we'll be as warm
as if we were fast asleep in our own brown chalet.'
Clara was not so sure. 'I'm soaking wet
from all this snow. What if you haven't the strength
to make Fængler give up the wishing chain?'
'Trust me to find a way,' said Berwald. 'Now don't
Bother me. I am thinking.' And he fell asleep.
Then Clara heard a stir in the snow. Something
was casting it off with a tune of tinkling chimes.

IV

SNOWBELL & EDELWEISS

Who can predict whether a plant will be modest or proud?
There are some haughty spirits hiding out on high, cold slopes.
Edelweiss thinks HE's the most important upland inhabitant
since people climb icy rocks to find him clinging to steep cliffs
and greet his wool-grey flower as if it glittered like a jewel.
It suits him to be sought out and consulted like a sage.
Snowbell, often called Soldanella, who has to push aside
half-melted ice, makes a kind, mild-mannered companion
if you listen to the lilt of her violet-tassled petals.

-◆-

Clara stole out of their hollow. The moon
showed her a patch of snow punctured by
a tiny dark bell that shook with new life.
'Soldanella, what a surprise to find you here!'
*'I have shuffled off my snow-house to welcome
summer'*, replied the flower valley-dwellers thought
brave and gentle, enduring late snows without a complaint.
Clara was hungry, afraid of wolves, and longed for home
but tried to sound strong. 'Berwald is growing up fast
and we're off to take the lucky silver chain
from Fængler.' Soldanella chimed loudly.
Perhaps she was amused, astonished or both.
*'So many have failed. Plans are not the way.
Fængler can only be foiled if you make
the Rose-hearted wish, the purest kind
whose power is at the heart of everything.
Wishing that will make him a weak old man.'*
'How easy just to make a wish!' laughed Clara.

At this Soldanella almost jangled out of tune.
*'To make a truly rose-hearted wish is easier
and harder than taking an axe to your enemy,
and no one can tell you how. All other ways
only SEEM to crush the cunning of evil.'*
'So who can help us?' Clara felt defeated.
*'Lady Alpenrose perhaps. She can sense
what kind of wish you are making. But she's
rarely seen and even less so in recent years.'*
'Then what are we to do?' Soldanella's next
advice felt like another long way round.
*'You might consult the woolly Edelweiss.
Living so high up with all that time to think
and such wide views, he should be wise.
You'll find him beyond that crag, living
in a cleft between two grey rocks. He knows
the best way to reach Fængler's cave.
Be polite. He's used to respect from visitors.'*

Sunlight woke the children to an unknown place.
They washed away sleep in a stream and ate
wild berries. Soldanella's advice meant little
to Berwald. He'd cut a heavy stick with his
forest knife. What use were rose-hearted wishes?
'At least let's find the Edelweiss,' begged Clara.
'Very well,' he said. 'But don't expect me
to make that wish.' 'You can't,' she insisted.
'First you have to discover what it is.'

Descending the mountain side showed them
the world beyond, stretching countless miles,
and a broad river snaking into misty distance.
Then they saw the Edelweiss in his niche
also taking in the view while he proudly
smoothed down his woollen cap and folded
his shawl of grey leaves about him until
he might be taken for a ball of grey velvet.
His jet-black eye was severe and penetrating
but he ignored the children, even Berwald,
who began to laugh at his comic appearance.
'He won't help us,' whispered Clara. 'Ha!Ha!
He's just a grey lump draped in a tatty cloak!'
jeered Berwald. 'Hi, Mr Woolly! Fine day!'
The flower seemed to look even further beyond them.
'We're wasting time on this knitted statue.'
Before Clara could check her brother, she heard
a high-pitched, creaky voice. Whose could it be?

'Who does that boy think he is? High time
he learnt to behave. He'll get nowhere fast
if he scoffs at his betters.' 'He meant no harm,'
said Clara. 'Why shouldn't I laugh?' shouted Berwald
who turned his back and flung himself down to rest.
'PLEASE, Mr Edelweiss,' Clara tried, still in hope.
'That's more like it. Please is much appreciated,'
squeaked the ruffled plant, staring hard at her.
'Can you tell me how to make the *rose-hearted* wish?'

'Nonsense!' came the reply. 'Listen to one
who knows. That won't get you anywhere.
Only the GREY wish provides my fine colour
and high position. How do you think I got here?'
'Did birds or kindly spirits lift you?' 'More nonsense!'
Edelweiss turned shrill and crackly, tapping
his head and holding it high. 'Look at this!
It's full of hard-earned knowledge. I suppose
you've been listening to some vain, brainless flower.'

Grey could never be better than rose, thought Clara;
but Berwald broke in with:- 'How can I wish
the grey wish? I want to get on.' 'That insulting
little boy has woken up!' snorted the flower,
fixing him with a cold stare. 'First learn manners,
then aim high, as I have done, and put yourself first.
Don't waste wishes on helping others along.'
'I despise the grey wish', said Clara. 'I want
to return father's flocks and give mother the silver
chain to bless us all. You are selfish and stuck up.'
'So much for good advice,' hissed the Edelweiss.
'Children never show respect.' 'Some love
their parents and feel thankful for their home,'
said Clara tearfully. And she ran down on to
flower-filled meadows below the grizzly crags.
As she flew along flecks of rose and gold sparkled
in her dress and tinged her shoes and stockings.
Without knowing she'd begun a *rose-hearted* wish.

Edelweiss thinks HE's the most important upland inhabitant since people climb icy rocks to find him clinging to steep cliffs and greet his wool-grey flower as if it glittered like a jewel.

V

THINK RED

*The king of birds has a keen eye for prey and is quick to kill
but war-lords of old worshipped him as warrior of the air,
befriended his families made them feel at home among men.
His children bore hero-names and knew when they were needed.
Legends recall birds of great size, loyal allies and lethal enemies
who rescued riders from ambush and restored outnumbered troops.
They learnt ways to boast and taunt, still ready on the tongues
of descendents driven off long ago to nest on deserted crags.
Hunters and herdsmen shot them for stealing game and harrying flocks.*

Berwald needed to ask more about the grey wish.
'Will it make me grow up more quickly?'
'Yes, and grow old,' chuckled the Edelweiss.
'I don't want that! How about other wishes?'
asked Berwald. 'You could try the fearful red wish,'
said the flower with a mocking smile the boy missed.
'That would force a way into Fængler's realms.
But you must consult the eagle who is proud
to have turned red from his years of cruelty.
He prefers young goats to boys but take care
he does not pounce on you.' 'I'll look out
for him,' said Berwald uncomfortably. 'Sorry
I laughed at you to begin with but you seemed
far too small to be of such importance.'
Another offence the flower decided to overlook.
'You'll learn that size does not always count.
Fængler is no bigger than a dwarf but look
at his power. And don't forget the grey wish.'

Berwald followed Clara downhill but not at a run,
and never wondered what might be happening
to his sister. Grey wishes weighed him down.
And he was so busy searching for the greedy
hawk he missed the array of wise, helpful
flowers that embroidered every step he took,
unaware that his shirt and socks and even
his brown curls were threaded with strands of grey.
Then a shadow passed over the sun and he saw
a vast pair of wings and a square tail wheeling
above him. He ran here and there waving his arms
till curiosity got the better of the proud bird
who made for a thorn bush that clung to a crag.
It bent and rocked as he sharpened his bill
on a gnarled branch, then swivelled his sharp eyes
to discover who or what had dared distract him.
Facing this presence with its cutting gaze, the boy
could not get beyond: 'Oh, please….Oh, thank you…'

Eagles have no patience. Luckily for Berwald
a beetle with a glistening green back whispered
from a rock: 'Ask him about himself.'
'Thank you,' said the boy, trying to clear his throat.
'Eagle…majestic Eagle, why do you look so red? '
The bird levelled his beak at him like a long knife
but he liked to brag about his fine appearance.
'I'm red with the blood of my easy prey,
Red with the early sun that lights my day.
Red with the blood of those who bar my way.
Red with the thought of what I can slay.'
His eyes caught fire with each red thought
and his voice reminded Berwald of something
being torn apart. How he wished his sister
stood beside him when the eagle sized him up
with his red eye. To sound sure of himself
he said: 'I am older than I look. I'm off
to take the lucky silver chain . I wish….'

'Make your wish clear, then,' rasped the eagle.
'My time is short and you are not good prey.
I once tried child flesh. It's disgustingly tough.'
'My mother calls me *as tough as old boots,*'
stammered Berwald. 'But the Edelweiss told me
to consult you about the Red Wish.
It's how to overcome Fængler and grow up fast.'
'Quick off the mark, aren't you?' muttered the eagle,
preening some stray feathers. 'Now guess *my* age!'
Berwald felt it didn't matter and he didn't care.
'I couldn't begin to.' 'Well, I'm the age of my beak
and slightly older than my wings. Caught you there!
Ageing eagles never number their years. Mind you,
my mountain pool mirror shows me I'm still trim.
As for that wish, how come your mother
let you loose with such bloodthirsty thoughts?'
'She didn't,' snapped Berwald, taking the eagle's tone,
'But I'll be back with power and a promise of riches.'

'The Red Wish will bring you both. Gray is feeble!'
pronounced the eagle. 'What about the rose-hearted wish?'
asked Berwald, not knowing why. The eagle
turned his beak up as high as it would go,
making Berwald feel small and stupid. 'Useless!'
shrilled the Eagle. 'Think red, wish red
to make sure no one else's wishes will succeed,
and do that all the way to Fængler's vaults.'
To add weight to this lesson he spread his wings
until they gleamed scarlet in the sun. Suppose
he flew off and left no directions, feared Berwald .
'How do I find my way? Is wishing red enough?'
'It could be!' The bird seemed amused. 'Look for
the watch tower beyond those rocks. Make sure
you mention me when you talk to the guards.
Depending on their mood they may let you in.'
He took off with a scream of mocking laughter
and darkened the rock face with a menacing shadow.

Berwald felt foolish and unsure of his plans.
He could not see what there was to joke about.
He found Clara lying beside some gentians,
calm and contented from what they had told her.
'Berwald, I may be nearer to understanding what
the rose-hearted wish means and how to make it.'
He put his hands over his ears. 'Don't confuse me.
I'm wishing grey to get the necklace myself, red
because Fængler's near and no one else must reach him.'

VI

Clipetty Clopitty

Trocktal's a high, narrow valley, an unhappy hideout,
its mouth protected by turreted walls and a tall spy tower.
Fængler's said to have faked the castle of a fine lady
he once loved. She led him on and left him for another.
Once admitted no one ever returns through this entrance.
Secret ways are kept secure to serve the stunted thief
on moonless nights when he makes his way below the mountain.
Relentless fear rules here and runs the lives of his slaves,
all grim except the gaping guardians of the battlements.

-◆-

Fængler's spy tower gleamed white against
a darkly forested valley. Limestone walls stretched
either way like arms open wide to forbid entrance.
The children would be watched winding their way
up a long stony track to the spiked oak gates.
Then a shuddering crash would lock them in.
But Berwald closed his mind to fear. He must
enter at all costs. Shielding his eyes he made out
two squat, square figures on the walls. They seemed
to be waiting for his next move. Clara hoped guards
would befriend children. 'Walk behind me,'
ordered Berwald. 'And keep your wishes quiet.'
'But just think of old Fængler,' she said.
'Shut away in that dull, dry valley.'
Some nearby pines sighed in a sudden breeze
and a clump of alpenrose burst into flower.
The guards took cover behind their walls
weakened by such long-forbidden kindness.

But hearing Berwald's firm stride and the scrape
of his stout stick, they felt the colour of his wish,
revived, and poked their ugly faces over the parapet.
Their heads were like boxes once empty, now
filled with mechanical parts. Their ears seemed
stuck on, and when they spoke their mouths gaped
so wide they nearly sliced away their heads.
'What do you want?' giggled one as if he'd cracked
a joke.' 'Food for a start', shouted Berwald, sick
of berries and ready to eat stale bread. The sentries
laughed until you could see the back of their throats.
'*WE* need the food that's here,' one managed to say
before he joined the other in howling with mirth.
Berwald tried to look as if he hadn't noticed
'Is this the way to visit Fængler?' he demanded.
'*Could* be,' said one. ' Shouldn't use it', said the other.
'I'm here to take it. And who are you two anyway?'
'Wants to know a lot!' they said with a wide smirk.

'I'm Clipetty', said one. 'I'm Clopitty,' said the other.
'Does that ring a bell?' 'Yes!' said Clara to please them.
We sing about you as we roll along in a cart.
> *Clipetty Clopitty Clop*
> it's ever so slow
> making our way to the top,
> then down we go,
> oh so fast we'll never be able to stop.
> *Clopitty Clipetty Clop*

But I've never met Clop.' Which made them laugh
so loudly their heads must surely be cut in two.
Then Clipetty said: 'I'm afraid it's different here:
> *Clipetty Clopitty Stop*
> you've come too far too fast.
> If we let you past
> it'll be *chipetty-chop*
> and you'll be cooked for breakfast!
> *Clopitty Clipetty Stop.*

Not nice! Hadn't you better go back the way you came ?'
'First we intend to take the lucky chain.'
Berwald stood firm. 'So please open up.'
'O the wishing chain! I see!' mouthed Clipetty
as if surprised. 'Ye-es!!' giggled his brother.
'So many after it, aren't there, Clipetty!
And all so disappointed. They just won't listen.
> *Clipetty Clopitty Stop*
> You won't be the last
> to come riding a wish for the top
> if only we'd let you get past.
> But the wily old boss works fast
> and won't be persuaded to stop
> till he's drawn every bolt and made you quite fast.
> *Clopitty Clipetty Clack'*

Was this less silly than it seemed, Clara wondered.
She thought of mother at her spinning wheel,
her baby brother in his carved cradle, and spoke out.

'We must learn about the *rose-hearted* wish
before we return.' At once the guards ducked
out of sight and felt very weak till Clipetty
did his best to restore their strength like this:
> *'Clipetty Clopitty Clack*
> You'd better be turning back.
> In the Master's dale, my dear,
> the wrong-coloured wish
> goes down like a poisoner's dish.
> We've no room for roses here.
> *Clopitty Clipetty Clear'*

'But some people must have their own way,'
said Clipetty. Bolts clattered and the children
watched the gates of Dry Dale open. Stepping
into the cold vaults of the spy tower they heard
the great oak doors grind together and lock them in.
One guard led, the other shuffled and panted behind.
They passed nothing but stone walls and low arches.

Clara thought of home and its warm, carved comforts.
Then she noticed pictures of mountain scenes,
not knowing that these could change to give
orders to the guards or upset passing captives.
One showed the very place she longed for,
its glowing fire, the cradle nearby and dinner
on the table, though no one was sitting there.
Adam and his wife stood staring through the window
and the baby was crying. 'I wish we'd never
run away,' she said, almost to herself.
'If only we could all be happy and kind, even poor,
old…' '*Don't!!*' shouted the guards together.
'Watch what you wish. *Don't* get rose-hearted.
Here we *don't* even mention the idea of it.
Don't let Fængler suspect you know about it.'
'She doesn't,' scoffed Berwald. 'Let's get on…
We must be back with our prize before sunset.'
'Aha!! Good for you!' Yelled the box-heads.

'You'll certainly wish what's best for you.'
'What's the use of other wishes?' asked the boy.
'None at all,' agreed the brothers, nudging each other
as they unbarred a faint track under dense trees.
No flowers grew there. No light seeped through.
Far off a wolf howled. The children turned back
to find the gate shut, and behind it laughter
as bolts clicked in place. Berwald blamed the eagle
for bad advice. They were trapped in this wood
where Fængler lived and set out on his nightly rounds.
Here every spirit and living thing obeyed him.
'How I wish…' began Clara. 'Wishes mislead us,'
said Berwald. 'If you grow up quickly will you
carry me home? I'm so tired', sighed Clara.
Her brother threw down his stick and sprawled out
on the hard, dry, needled floor of the forest.
Clara knelt to comfort him. 'Fængler may be
kinder than they say….' He had fallen asleep.

Second Part

In Shadow

VII

FÆNGLER SURPRISED

The charmed wishing chain was no toy for a child
but anyone might wield it wisely for its true work.
Four right stones, four left, the fifth above the breast.
Eight held in their hearts a splinter finely hewn
from the one they faced to even out their power,
while the breast jade bore rose quartz in a nine-beamed star.
And each stone was locked in silver lace with nine links between,
ninety from hasp to hasp, all no heavier than a lock of hair,
tied by a steel catch and fit for testing in a tug of war.

Clara dreamed she'd taken Clipetty's dinner
but left it behind. She woke under pitch black
trees that refused to admit pale star light
or the waxing moon who tried so hard to pry.
Leaving her brother asleep she crept back to
the forest path, daring herself to see where it led,
explore places ruled by old Fængler's wishes.
Thick needles muffled her steps. Nothing stirred
under dense pines. Then far down the track
a light flickered, grew brighter and began to dance.
Someone must be swinging it and coming her way.
Who would tramp through this darkness
but the terrible figure they feared and hated?
Perhaps he was setting out to haunt their valley.
She made for the nearest pine and squeezed herself
behind its trunk, trembling but still determined
to snatch a glimpse of the twisted old trickster
whose evil ways they'd left home to overcome.

Just for a moment the moon found its way
through the canopy of pines and helped the lantern
light up a dumpy old man, almost as broad
as he was tall, whose triple-striding boots gave
him feet like flippers. His stomach bulged beyond
a shabby leather jacket, and a broad-brimmed hat
overshadowed his eyes and forehead. Most fearful
was the bushy beard that bristled all over his face
and hung like half-thawed icicles down to his knees.

Clara could hardly breathe but she remembered
the necklace. Would it shine with a light of its own?
By chance one curious moonbeam slipped
past a dead branch and touched the enchanter's chest.
There gleamed the lucky chain with its power
to bless or weigh down the wearer with his wishes.
Something made her lean forward and find herself
whispering: 'Oh, I wish…I wish…' Fængler stopped
in his tracks, looked her way listening hard, dropped

his lantern, snatched it up and ran back the way he'd come,
crying out in his cracked old voice 'Someone's
making wishes!' 'Yes! It's me!' shouted Clara,
amazed at herself as she chased him down
the dark, hushed avenue, darting behind pine trunks
to keep out of sight. *She* would find out where
the thief lived and beat Berwald to their goal.
Soon the wood gave way to a towering rock face,
and below it yawned a cave mouth lit by oil lamps.

One sentry stood there still trembling after
his master's angry return as if he were to blame.
His face reminded Clara of Clipetty and Clopitty
but it was stiff and unsmiling, and unlike them
he was all skin and bone inside his shoddy coat.
Seeing a girl follow Fængler from the forest
was another shock: he needed strict routine.
In panic he dropped his gun. 'You can't go further,'
he stammered. 'The master's so ill-tempered
he'd eat you if he had the teeth. It's my duty
to shoot those who disobey, though I'm not good
with guns and I might even shoot myself.'
Clara picked up his gun, held it muzzle upwards
and gently gave it back. 'Handling that is risky,'
he said. 'I fear guns as much as old Fængler.'
Clara said brightly: 'I often clean father's gun.'
Then sadly: 'Will I see him and mother again?'
'Your fault if you don't. Why come to this place?'

The solemn little man sounded like a schoolteacher.
'No one here knows how to smile,' he droned on.
'Except those silly outpost sentries. Though there is
the Bright Beetle. Only *she* can do it here
but she has to practise hard. I don't suppose
you ever saw a beetle smile.' 'No. I'd love to,'
said Clara. 'She smiles out loud. Try and stop her!
She reminds me of you.' As he said this
a faint twinkle lit the ragged guard's eyes.

'If only I could meet her!' said Clara. 'Not to smile
must be dreadful. Where I live we do it without trying.
I'm sorry for you all. I'd like to…' 'Stop!!'
he commanded more in fear than anger.
'Rose-hearted feelings have not been uttered
here since these ranks of trees were planted.
We've no use for such behaviour.' 'But I want
to know how to wish like that,' she said. 'Everyone
seems to know about it. I begin and never finish.'

'May I look inside old Fængler's cave ? It's so quiet!
Is he asleep?' 'You'll take the consequences,'
warned the guard. Clara felt her heart beat and her breath
come fast but said: 'I like consequences.
I take them because they make adventures.'
Risks disturbed him. 'You can have too much
of a good thing.' But her eyes shone like gentians
set alight at dawn as she crossed the grim threshold
into the rock chamber where a brazier blazed
and smoked right in the centre. Fængler liked smoke:
it upset prisoners and servants. He sat hunched
before the fire, elbows on knees, his beard trailing
on the damp stone floor. Clara saw and forgot
the chain round his neck when she noticed how
his long nose and chin nearly met. She waited
for him to turn from the fire and fix her with his eyes.
Then he coughed so loudly she jumped forward and saw
something glisten on his beard. Could it be a tear?

Whatever trickled there, Clara suddenly met
her grandfather in that wretched old scarecrow.
He loved and welcomed children, and she longed
so much to see him, why not run and throw
her arms around the gloomy hermit? 'He's so unhappy,
so lonely and old!' Her voice echoed round the cave.
'He has driven everyone away and will never know
kindness again. I'm beginning to fear him less
and pity him so much more.' As she spoke

all the smoke vanished and the fire leapt up
with rose-coloured flames. Trees outside burst
into light and danced with chains of twinkling roses.
A rosy sunrise seemed to flood the cave. Fængler
had nowhere to hide. He looked confused and weak.
Clara did not know what power she wielded in
wishing to comfort the outcast, or how her warm
heart made this barren place clothe itself in rose.
Nor could she seize her chance to take the lucky chain.

Just for a moment the moon found its way
through the canopy of pines and helped the lantern
light up a dumpy old man, almost as broad
as he was tall…..

VIII

DEEPER & DARKER

*When Fængler's darkened soul drove him to depart
from where his skill in woodland crafts was well-received,
the upper dale was ravaged by diggings and riddled with tunnels.
He made himself master, manipulated the last of the miners
who lived by sifting precious ores from sparse seams,
and bared the land of tree and bush to burn in their smelting.
He had them plant pines and prepare his cunning defences,
summoned back forest spirits and put them to service.
So years of filth were flushed from his cavernous fortress.*

Clara stood there delighted by the rosy glow
that overpowered the crooked old man so long
as noone broke the spell. How could she tell
her time had come to take the wishing chain?
A loud shouting from the woods broke into the cave,
and heavy footsteps followed. 'Clara! Clara!
You've left me behind! But I'll get even. You won't
get the necklace. I intend to have it. No one else
will beat me to it.' Berwald waking cold and hungry
came rampaging down the forest path, putting out
the joyous lights he never noticed. The fire's rosy
flames withered into sickly yellow and gave out
bitter smoke. At once the trembling old cheat
turned into Fængler the fearful, striding across
the rocky floor in his swift boots, his face creased
with the hatred of one who has feared for his life.
This was when Clara first saw and felt the force
of eyes that glinted with cruel orange fire.

Wishing **red** Berwald released and strengthened countless
spiteful woodland spirits who served Fængler in fear
and like him had slunk away from rosy light.
They taunted him with: 'Ho-ha-ho!! Wouldn't you like
to get it for yourself!' 'I will. You'll see,' he shouted.
'The Red Eagle has shown me how and sent me here.'
They mocked him even more. 'Oh the **Red One**!
He never lies and what a friend he is to Fængler!
Feeds him fat young boasters just for fun!'
Linking up they locked him in with ever–shifting
chains, and the more he struggled the tighter
they fastened their untouchable links with ugly
chuckles that drowned his cries to be freed
and sent home. Clara watched in fear. Fængler grinned
as the web's threads thickened. Angry with the Eagle
and this torment Berwald wished red again and again
and closed the trap. Clara shouted through the jeers:
'Berwald! Why have you come here wishing **red**?'

Just when old Fængler might have turned kind
and I began to think I might like him, and…'
She broke off stunned by how the spirits froze
and almost faded while their master looked ready
to shrink into his boots. Then Berwald shouted:
'I'm going to get the chain, grow up and be rich…'
'Aha! That's your tune, is it!' snarled Fængler,
who leapt at them in one stride, grabbing Clara's hair
with one hand and Berwald's with the other.
Small and fat as he was he had the strength
of a demon, forcing them on at a great pace.
Clara in her fear could only wish they were safe
in their chalet. Her brother kicked, dragged
his feet, and made lunge after lunge at the necklace.
This was worse than being trapped by spirits.
Fængler clutched like a vice. Every forest
spirit danced about them and croaked in mockery.
The solemn guard waited for orders, his gun upside down.

The captives were marched further and deeper into
a network of rocky passages. Even the servants
could not tell where Fængler in his fury
would take these helpless children. His lock-ups
were hard to find and only he knew their exits.
As Berwald's tired legs were forced on at a trot,
and he felt as if steel pincers tugged at the roots
of his hair, he lost courage and his red thoughts.
Soon the yelping procession of ugly dancers
fell back and only the solemn guard followed,
gun under one arm, mirror that showed his orders
half-out of one pocket. He carried the lantern
Fængler had not long before dropped in shock
at feeling Clara's wishes in his private forest.
Reflecting rage its hollowed oak glowed orange
or ghostly turquoise when sudden draughts caught it.
The guard shivered in fear but set his face to frown
like a grim servant and to suit old Fængler's mood.

At last they reached a door made of nine tree trunks
bound and framed with iron. A little bearded hunchback
leapt up to turn a two-handled key with all his strength,
opening up a wall of darkness that made the passage
look like twilight. Into this cavern the heartless bully
hurled the children by their hair like dead plants.
'That's where you go for trying to take the lucky chain,'
he roared. 'It leads to the Unlucky Dell.
Climb and scramble day and night. You won't tell
which and you won't find a way out.
And from outside there's no way in.
So it's no use anyone hoping to find you.
Think yourselves lucky if someone brings you
dirty water and stale bread or a bone to gnaw.'
The dwarfish key guard gave out a harsh chuckle,
the nearest Fængler's people got to laughter, swung
the nine trunks into place and heaved back the locks.
The captives stumbled forward clinging together in fear.

Then they heard a familiar noise. 'Hark!' whispered Berwald.
'Doesn't that come from home?' asked Clara. 'Yes. It might
belong to Ladybrown.' Berwald sounded less hoarse.
'Father's best milk and mothering cow. It's her bell.
The old prowler muffled it to drive her away.
If only it *is* her! She might know the way out.'
From nowhere a sombre voice said: 'Way out!
No such thing! And no one returns through the cave.'
'It's the solemn guard!' said Clara. 'Ladybrown *and* you!
It's not so bad!' She reached for the hand that still
held the lantern. Its fitful yellow suddenly flamed
deep pink because the guard's enslaved heart
squeezed out a little kindness towards the captives.
That brief rosy beam showed them two gates, one open
to a track that dropped into a sheer-sided dell
from which the cow bell had tinkled. The other
was padlocked. Beyond its spike-topped palings loomed
a wood twice as dense as the one before the cave.

IX

DEAD WOOD

*Before Fængler came and cleared the mines, meadows clung to the hillside
and stretched for miles. Below them streams broke from sheer rock
and tumbled in tuneful cascades to the tilled valley below.
Now Dead Wood runs on and on where herds roamed over rich pasture.
Waste and rock wheeled and scattered over the well-watered shelf
spilt over steep ledges and massed in a slope of weedy sludge,
blocking the buoyant waters that blessed the dale and made it lush.
Pines in thousands were planted, thrived and grew tall only to perish.
Then mountain clematis crept in and covered the wreck with its webs.*

'That Unlucky Dell is not for me,' said Berwald,
looking into the dark hollow where Ladybrown
now sounded further off. 'What chance will I have
of getting the lucky chain if I'm down there?'
'You've no chance anyway,' said the guard
in his solemn tone. 'Fængler's more than cruel.
He's cunning. Loopholes are closed and gates guarded.'
'What about that other gate?' asked Clara.
'Hush!' warned the guard. 'That's *Dead Wood*
behind it, and no one walks among its dead pines.
No plants grow. No creatures are at home.
Only thick creepers thrive, draining the land dry
and banishing light with drapes like dirty cobwebs.
Now and again a robin tries to sing but only
because he likes to flavour his songs with sadness
before leaving.' 'Might he come today?' asked Clara.
'He chooses his times,' said the guard mournfully
as if talking about the robin's song saddened him.

'What about you? Can you leave?' asked Clara.
'I don't know. My mirror will tell me.'
'Will it tell us?' Berwald sounded down-hearted.
'I don't know,' said the guard. 'I doubt it.
And I don't think you will ever get out.'
'Isn't it time we had something to eat and drink?'
demanded Berwald. 'I don't know' was the answer.
'You don't seem to know anything! What's your name?'
This hurt the solemn guard and he said nothing.
Clara nudged her brother and whispered: 'Don't offend him.'
But he shouted: 'I need to get out and soon.'
'First learn some respect', said the guard severely.
'Even then you would find it too hard or too far.'
'Father will come searching', said Clara brightly.
'No one finds a way into the Unlucky Dell.
People are put there for meddling with old Fængler.'
The guard's words were like the dead end they'd reached.
'Your lantern's out,' said Berwald. 'Dare I ask if you can light it?

'I don't know how,' said the guard, taking out
his mirror to find instructions. It was as dark
as where they stood. Then he heard Clara cover
up a sob as she wished they'd never left home
or followed this fool's chase for a necklace.
For Berwald he felt no pity. He'd seen boys
here before. All full of themselves. He hated
guarding captives in this dark place where
he was hungry and confused about his work.
But hearing Clara hide her misery made him
feel something new he could not explain
and did not like. He suspected anything new.
It was sorrow for Clara sending a secret
wish into his heart: if only he could help
her escape the clutches of his evil master!
'Look at the lantern!' cried Berwald. 'It's burning
pink again. Suppose I wish red, will it flame
bright red and show us a way out of here?'

The guard looked down again and saw no more
than a shape in his hand. 'You have put it out,
you thoughtless boy,' he said in a calm voice.
'I never touched it,' said Berwald. 'You don't light
such lanterns by touch', said the weary guard. 'It's done
by thinking and only if you learn to think the right thoughts.'
'Perhaps it could light our way to supper or tea.
I've lost all track of time,' said Clara feeling weak
with hunger. 'Here there's only breakfast,' said her guard.
'And you've missed that. A brief crimson glow
sometimes lends a little light to this shadowy place.
Snowy mountains to the east reflect the low sun.
That tells you the time but you can't eat it.
Oh and here's the robin,' continued the dull voice.
'He'll probably perch on the gate to Dead Wood
if you want to hear him sing.' Clara pulled Berwald
forward. They heard a rustle, some questioning notes,
then a song that felt both tearful and determined.

Clara still knew the language of birds. Berwald
had almost lost touch with it. She explained
how the robin's song told of their valley,
how Father Adam had set out after their first
night away, armed with staff and axe, intent
on never returning home without his children.
Then, as the guard had foreseen, a maroon
radiance showed through Dead Wood beyond
pines that crowded in dense columns round the gates.
'Ah!' exclaimed Clara, always ready to hope,
'This light and the robin's message should cheer us.'
'Joy is not respectable here. Don't show it!'
ordered the guard. (Trouble might come from her words.)
'I'm not respectable', she said. 'Nor is Robin.'
' O dear Robin show us how to meet father!'
The bird shook his beak, put his wise head
on one side and stared from his piercing eye,
though they only saw him as a shadowy outline.

'First you must light   the oak lantern.
Put in the back   of a black beetle,
a bird's feather   found or freely given,
wing of a firefly   wronged or wounded,
one curl of your hair   no matter its colour.
Distil among these   three drops of dew,
though rarely found   in this ravaged wood.
Add a tear of someone   who feels true sorrow.
Then kindle a spark.   How, I cannot say.'
Clara explained and the guard mumbled: 'Spark! My mirror
never shows such a thing.' 'Feathers!' scoffed Berwald.
'That robin's the only bird to visit *and* rarely!'
The bird heard this clearly and sang to Clara:
You may take a feather   from my tail.
Don't pick the largest   or pull too suddenly.
Little ones hurt me   but very much less.
You're welcome to choose   whatever your chances.
I never say no   if I see there's a need.

'Seems to repeat himself a lot,' said Berwald,
only grasping a little of what the robin sang.
But its words kindled pink lights that hung
from the wood's dead branches beyond the gate,
reminding Clara of her early morning escapade
when Fængler's cave and forest filled with rosy light.
The robin appeared as he would in broad daylight,
and she walked up to his perch and plucked a small
feather from his tail. 'Thank you, robin. Your heart
is so kind.' Berwald grunted thanks ungraciously.
The guard shivered. What if Fængler found out?
He'd get the blame. The robin bowed in reply,
though noone saw him, for the lights had faded.
'I visit briefly   and seldom venture back.
I'll soon be in your valley   singing the sun down.
I'd urge your father on   only he's forgotten the tongue.
I wish you well   and a quick welcome home.
Get through to the wood   by the gate's third spike.'

Without pause for thanks the children rushed to
test the pailings. The third from where the robin perched
was loose. He'd watched Fængler creep through at dusk
to reach a secret exit for his evil wanderings.
Berwald wrenched up the spike and they crawled in.
The trembling guard followed, dragging his lantern and gun.
'We'll soon be out!' Berwald felt sure. Clara wondered
how to avoid Clipetty and Clopitty. 'You won't!'
said their warder. 'The master's sentinels are sharp.
You'll have to find a way that avoids the battlements.
First you need a firefly and a beetle, hard enough
without expecting to find dew and tears as well.'
'You find what you're after,' said Berwald boldly.
As night thickened, their third away from home,
the wood enclosed them with its gloomy creepers.
They shuffled through deep layers of dead needles
shed by pines that had taken many years to die.
Any moment Fængler might give chase or set a trap.

X

FÆNGLER'S LANTERN

*The robin's remedy for relighting the oaken lamp
spoke of a serious loss in this starved land
where Fængler had far outstripped other forest folk
in cutting close ties with long-loved companions.
Most befriended the great beetle for battling with woodland pests,
and felt sure of summer growth where glittering fireflies gathered.*

*When fleece or feather are given freely as the blessing of dew,
light fed from such fuel but fortified by sorrow
will overwhelm evil and erase darkness.*

A walk through Dead Wood was no easy stroll.
They blundered into creepers thick as a man's thigh,
plunged down sudden rocky hollows and dry dykes.
How long had they trekked like this, looking
in vain for fireflies, beetles or a broad leaf
that might cup a drop of dew? Berwald broke
a long silence with: 'Suppose I take the lantern.'
'Expecting it to shine pink for you?' sneered the guard.
'I don't want it to and I don't trust that bird's
recipe. Have you got its feather?' He asked Clara,
holding on to the robin's words after all.
As she took it from her handkerchief and touched it
tenderly a slight breeze seemed to shift
the wood's black curtains and something bright scuttled
past Clara's feet. It was a firefly in a hurry.
'Short cuts never work. I'm on my way
to meet my beetle friend who waits outside
these dreary, dried-up realms that weigh me down.'

At first Berwald heard only breathless squeaks.
'Tread on it!' he yelled. And something like a howl
sounded far behind. 'Is that a wolf?' he asked.
'No!' said the guard. 'Fængler's folk were cheering.'
'Can they *hear* me?' Fear trickled down his back.
'No. They simply felt you,' came the reply.
'Clara, we do need a wing.' The boy wouldn't give in.
'I'll protect her', she said. 'The fly's meeting someone
she may love dearly and who's concerned for her.'
'That's all true, and he dislikes me cutting
through this wood to meet him,' said the firefly.
'But we also want to leave this wood behind,
and we can't unless we light this oaken lamp.
We need a firefly's wing and a beetle's back.'
'My wings are mine. My friend's a handsome beetle.'
'Could your friend give us advice?' asked Clara.
'Probably. He warned me off this wood.
And here I am without much time in hand.'

The tongue was coming back to Berwald. 'Why not
listen? This is no place for anyone alive.'
'Do you always take advice?' asked the firefly.
'Sometimes your own ideas may seem the best.'
He had no answer, and Clara asked kindly: 'May we
follow you?' *'As you wish,'* the fly replied.
As her little light rippled along, the wood seemed
less dead and it helped them on, though often
children and guard crawled on hands and knees.
'We'll never have to cross this wilderness again!'
said Clara with joy when at last they saw
moonlight beyond Fængler's boundaries, inviting
them down a colonnade of living pines where
even a few leafy trees and shrubs could thrive.
Ahead lay a row of high rough-hewn palisades,
then a rocky slope, perhaps the shoulder of a mountain
whose other side looked down on their home.
'Our valley lies just beyond!' shouted Clara.

'Don't be noisy!' advised the guard. 'We're *here* not there.'
'Light that lantern,' said Berwald. 'Then we'll find father.
You've treated us well so you may come along too.'
'I'll have to think about that,' said the guard.
'The lantern's still out. All in good time.'
'Here's my beetle friend!' exclaimed the firefly.
'Yes, my dear, I know you're angry with me.
I risked a short way through but I'm here!
These children almost took my precious wings,
but the kinder of the two prevailed.'
'You don't know how relieved I feel,' said the beetle,
who was a neat little creature, though he looked
upset and very pale despite his perfect sheen.
'Here's a tragic sight to hurt your eyes.
Look! It breaks my heart to think of it.'
They all peered through a barred and padlocked gate
at a heap of cast off firefly wings and beetle backs.
Insects added relish to Fængler's main meal.

Both children almost shouted with delight,
then they thought how the sight would strike the insects.
The firefly drooped her wings. The beetle tried to
console her. Both wanted to leave but he asked
if they could be of help before they made for safety.
'I gather Fængler's lantern must be lit
for you to leave the wood. I'll brave
that terrible pile to fetch the wing and back you need.
If you meet the Bright Beetle on your travels,
ask her for advice. You'll find she's not quite
what she seems...' 'Time's short,' broke in Berwald.
How about the drops of dew?' The beetle replied:
'That acorn by your feet would hold a few
from rose leaves outside Fængler's dried up land.
You won't find dew where darkness has its way,
and crying there is just as hard as laughter.'
'Clara will cry alright,' said Berwald. The beetle
stared knowingly and made him feel uneasy.

And then the kindly insect darted under the fence
with his acorn cup that was warped and old
but held the drops. He brought them back with a bow.
'We wish you luck,' he said. *'And don't forget*
the curl and tear. That robin is my friend.
He leaves beetles alone and goes for slugs.
I trust you've seen the last of Master Fængler.'
With that he escorted the still shocked and silent firefly
into green and living lands beyond this ruined wood.
'Now for that curl, Clara,' said Berwald. 'Last
ingredient but one.' 'How about yours?' she asked.
'Too short,' he said, feeling for his penknife.
Clara lost one of her most shining curls
and saw it mixed into the lantern's hold.
A tiny flame flickered but far too weakly
to light up the twisting tunnels of heavy creepers.
They needed the tear of a child who felt true sorrow.
'You'll cry soon won't you?' Berwald asked his sister.

'*I* can't cry. I'm too pleased with thinking how
once the lantern's alight we'll creep back to Fængler's cave
and make him give up the necklace. Then we can
set off to meet father and won't he admire us!
If you think of mother and baby all alone you'll cry.
But don't delay. We need the power of this light.'
'Why aren't we going straight home?' asked Clara.
Let's forget the chain and return to mother and baby.'
'I can't!' shouted her brother. 'And *I* can't cry,'
protested Clara. 'Of course not!' broke in the guard.
'Surely the beetle told you no one here laughs
or cries. Before Fængler life in the mines was grim
but he spread gloom to every living thing.
Once you're in his lands you can't show
joy or sorrow. He alone can light this lamp
with a spark from his evil eye.' They felt hopeless
and angry but no tears came. Then suddenly
their guard dropped the lantern and began to shake.

XI

THE MASTER'S POWER

The dale below Dead Wood was doomed and named Unlucky
after Fængler's ruinous plans turned farmland to fen
and torrents of sludge silted up the swift brooks.
Thorn and alder clustered and clung to humps in the clogged land,
robbing light from grass and herb where beasts once gathered to graze.
To drive and sort the stock filched as food for feckless slaves,
causeways were built to run criss-cross over the marsh.
Along their margins threadbare green made scant meals for lean beasts
kept through long winters on stolen fodder in cramped caves.

-◆-

'Why are you trembling?' asked Berwald, who thought
he heard the robin singing a song that mocked him.
Perhaps his anger sent the moon behind a cloud,
for the darkness suddenly felt closer and tighter.
'I heard something,' stammered the guard. 'A coward
after all!' shouted Berwald. Then came a commotion
like hundreds of light-footed creatures stampeding
through the wood, whatever stood in their way.
Fumbling for his mirror the guard shouted in panic:
They're coming for us, threw down the lantern
and vanished into a cleft between fallen pines.
With nowhere to hide the children clung together
as the hissing shuffle threw out a green mist
that lit up the broken trees and strangling creepers.
Then, his boots taking monstrous strides, and club in hand,
Fængler found them. His eyes gleamed and spat like fire
as he rumbled with wordless rage like a cornered
bull who threatens to crush everything in sight.

Clara was too rigid with fear to make a wish.
Berwald burned with red anger. 'You two again!'
growled the ugly tyrant. 'You belong in the dell
with my captive flocks on one meal a day.
Where's the guard and why's my lantern lying there?'
The guard heard this. Though his master's sight
was keen in good light, dark corners were safe.
And the children said nothing to betray him.
Berwald eyed the lantern but Fængler clawed it up,
dropped his club, grabbed and shook the boy:
'Now I'll make doubly sure you won't go home.'
A cruel glint from his eyes shot sparks into
the lantern that flared up to mirror his malice.
The precious recipe that lacked a tear of sorrow
melted into smoke along with every hope and plan.
Darting from their ghostly green mist a host
of Fængler's spirit slaves formed a dancing chain
about each captive, leering as their hold tightened.

Their grim master buckled the lantern to his belt
as he watched this mocking dance with a pitiless grin,
enjoying the boy's attempt to break the enchanted web.
He barked an order the children did not grasp,
and his gangs conjured up luminous cords
that bristled with lighted points. These they spiralled
round their victims from throat to waist in case
they tried to run and hide. Then they were hauled
back through the wood that took so long to cross,
their merciless jailer's wicked yellow lamp blazing
a trail ahead of his company's pale green light
till he reached the gate whose secret the robin revealed.
Here Fængler took a great key from his leather coat,
unlocked it without a click and had his captives dragged
towards the steep slope they'd seen before. It fell
over rock and scrub into the Unlucky Dell.
Clara felt sure she heard familiar cattle bells.
Her brother was too full of rage to listen or care.

'Stop!' shouted the leader. The mischievous crowd froze.
'Release!' Some took an end of each tightened
cord and with a sudden jerk spun the children
head over heels, and down they rolled at breakneck
speed over ledges, bruised by stones, their bare flesh
and clothes torn by briars and thorns, while the conjurer
stood among his host and watched, delighted to hear
cries of fear and pain growing fainter as the fall
knocked the breath out of his prey and they were lost
to sight among the shadows of the luckless dale.
At last they stuck fast in water-logged sedge,
wet through and aching in every bone and muscle.
'Clara, can you move?' gasped Berwald who felt
as if his limbs would never bend or carry him.
'It's a miracle our heads were not crushed.'
'I'm bruised all over,' moaned Clara. 'I'd gladly
roll Fengler's fat body over those stones.'
'And may wolves savage the Red Eagle,' said Berwald.

'Now we'll never see our family again.'
Clara rarely gave way to such despair
but their capture just at the edge of Dead Wood
had crushed her more than plunging into this pit.
The mountain glimpsed hours ago now hid
the moon, though it would be shining silver-clear
on their home. How was mother feeling, she wondered.
Somewhere in the gloom they heard cattle bells clang
and the jingle of goat collars. 'Ladybrown
must be there', said Clara, longing to greet a friend.
'Let's look for her!' 'I can hardly move,'
said Berwald. 'And I won't know what she's telling us.
There's no way out now. We'll grow old here.'
'No!' protested his sister. 'That means we'll forget
how to laugh.' She felt sure that Ladybrown
or even Parsnip the goat, would bring cheer and comfort.
When Clara called the cow remembered her voice
and they buried themselves in the warmth of her welcome.

Third Part

Rally

XII

ADAM'S SEARCH

*Maria had proved herself a patient wife and prudent mother,
mostly indoors for many days managing her home with skill
while Adam and their children were out among livestock or in the forest.
In youth she'd worked all weathers helping with welfare of cattle,
by her father's side at any hour attending to births or ailments.
Early she filled her heart with flower and forest lore,
resolved never to lose the wisdom she'd learned and loved.
Hearing the gift of tongues nature gave to guide her children,
she held more firmly to her own if only to seek help and healing.*

Here the tale returns to Adam and Maria
in the homely chalet, waiting for their children
while a long summer evening grew dim,
though Berwald and Clara had crossed the high eastern pass
and found by chance a safe cleft under the snow.
They had not returned for the midday meal
and now their parents looked at two empty chairs
round a table prepared for supper, the very picture
seen later on the walls of Fængler's fortress.

Now in this last glimmer of dusk Adam walked
forest paths calling his children home and only
nightingales answered as if nothing could ever
disturb their summer visit to thickets they loved.
He searched behind stacks of logs and into hollow
trees, and higher over rocky outcrops
where gentians and glossy-leaved alpenrose saw him
look at them, knowing he longed to ask for news.
If only his busy life had not banished their tongue!

He returned downhill in despair, wondering
if Fængler had spirited away his loved-ones.
He counted his goats and his brown cows that grazed
and tolled their bells in open meadows. None
were missing. If the dreaded thief had called
it was not for livestock. This time perhaps
he'd captured children out of spite or envy,
or was it some twisted scheme of bargaining?
Little ones had been taken for such purposes.

And when Maria heard his fears she went as still
and cold as stone, feeling more helpless
than her husband, since she must brood at home and keep
her baby free from sensing all their pain and trouble.
No sleep blessed that night. Adam rose early
to tend his herds, longing to wield the lucky necklace.
'Wouldn't I pay back and punish that evil hustler!'
Dawn seemed to stop brushing the forest crests,
and he recalled the howl of hungry winter wolves.

As his anger and fear grew, trees and mountains
loomed over him and he felt sure
his children suffered torments and might never be found.
Not once did he think his talk about the chain
had fired them to take such risks and please him.
Even now he insisted he would never
return without his children *and* the Wishing Chain.
'What is that trinket to us?' asked Maria
in sorrow as she rocked baby to sleep. 'The safe
return of our handsome Berwald and lovely Clara
is worth more than a thousand wishing gems.'
'Be strong and keep up your hopes!' said Adam,
drawing on his boots and choosing a staff and axe.
'Soon I'll be back to cheer you with *all three.*'
'May forest guardians and kindly flowers guide you over
more than choosing paths or where our children went,'
advised Maria. 'I'd rather trust my stout stick,'
replied Adam, waving farewell as he strode away.

Climbing beyond Mittelbach's playful waters
he saw Red Eagle perched on a crag,
spitting out a ball of feathers after his meal,
then proudly displaying his speckled scarlet wings.
Adam hunted eagles when they harassed flocks
and stole their young but hawk speech was close to his.
They were vain and cruel yet never missed a movement
in their hunting grounds. 'Have you seen children
pass this way?' asked the forester politely.

The eagle turned its back. 'A boy and a girl,'
Adam said more firmly. 'I'm going deaf,'
complained the eagle. 'It's useless to talk to me.'
'Have you seen my children in your murderous wanderings?'
Adam gripped his stick in anger. 'My eyesight
is not as sharp as it was. I might have done
but then of course I might not. I try to mind
my own business. Few seem able to do so.'
'True,' said the woodsman. 'But this is *my* business.'

'More likely your ill luck,' said the Red Eagle,
picking over a last scrap of prey. 'You brought
this trouble on yourself. You would keep talking
about the wishing chain.' 'You may be right,'
admitted Adam. 'But what have you seen today?'
'Birds are said to gossip about what they see or hear,'
said the eagle, his beak stuck up in contempt.
 'I'm different. Good day!' Lost for words,
Adam watched him spiral upwards at a great pace.

XIII

WELL-WISHER

No one was sure how long Lady Well-wisher had lived,
where light first blessed her or how she learned her lore.
Some held that in her youth she had a hand in making
the Necklace and knew how the nine stones were worked upon.
She alone felt joy touch or sorrow take its toll
on everything alive in all the dales for miles around.
What the heart said she prized. To ponder was power enough.
Many who confided in her felt they heard contráry counsel
then later found unloosed some inner source long untouched.

-◆-

Adam looked at his well-seasoned stick.
It felt useless. 'I'll consult the Well-wisher,
though she too may have little to say.'
This wise old lady (as most took her to be)
might have been born before the valley's oldest
trees were even saplings. Perhaps that's why
she understood their strange whisperings, a secret
wisdom they took from beams of the waxing moon.
She rarely spoke of this but along with all
she learnt from knowing every tongue, it went
into a great cast iron pot of dreams
that simmered day and night on her log hut fire.
She lived at the northernmost end of a long dale
where steep forest gave way to mountain rock.
Now and again she'd offer a sip from her pot
to anyone who called to enjoy her kindly smile
and quietly spoken wisdom or cures distilled
and taken before a fire she rarely seemed to stoke.

She favoured those who remembered forest speech
and earliest hopes, and took account of nightly dreams.
Aware of this, Adam doubted his welcome,
though something encouraged him to trudge all afternoon
and on into moonlight to reach her refuge.
Long before he toiled up the last tortuous
path and smelt her fire's smoky haze, he heard
in his head words and phrases of forest talk
quite unbidden. He'd no idea how or why.

Pausing to rest he'd been surprised to hear
a tuneful rustle long since foreign to his ears:
gentians saying they'd help him find his loved ones.
In the rose-red dawn (when miles away
to the south his children had entered Fængler's cave)
he found Well-wisher's weather-bleached hut
set between forest and flower-filled upland meadows,
her door open wide, for many kinds of message
aroused her interest in the woodsman's troubled journey.

Yet even when Adam looked in to greet her
she was too busy stirring her pot of dreams
to look up. Before dawn she'd mixed in
new dreams made of gold, petals, summer and love
that would be spoiled by careless handling. So Adam waited
a long while for her to look in his direction.
She turned, nodded remotely, paused to taste her mixture
and push the pot further on the fire. At last
she felt ready to entertain her visitor.

'I've been savouring some of my best dreams.
What can the old Well-wisher do for you?
You haven't come so far just to look at me!'
In fact her wise, age-worn face had a strange
beauty, and changed according to the light.
Her gown reminded Adam of springtime forest glades.
Her eyes were sharply aware yet softly amused,
and her forehead bore signs of deep dreaming.
Even gentians admired her subtle forest talk.

Adam removed his forester's hat that bore
in its band a dove's feather and alpenrose,
and bowed low to this loved and revered figure.
'I want to find my children and bring them home again,'
he said. 'They're missing and I don't know where to search.'
The Well-wisher stared at Adam as if she saw
through him or knew what he'd chosen not to say.
She turned round and took a long spoon to stir
her dreams. 'Don't you want the Wishing Chain as well?

I'm afraid the desire shines in your eyes!'
Adam blinked as if he was trying to hide
from her awareness. She saw this, too,
but sadly he must now face his worst fears.
'Berwald and Clara along with many of your beasts
are in the power of wicked master Fængler.
He'll pitch your children into Luckless Dale where sunlight
seldom shines, and joy and sorrow are forgotten.
There's no easy way to get them safely out.'

'You, of all folk in forest, field or mountain
can tell me how. I'm told and I believe
nothing's beyond your knowledge, my lady Well-wisher.'
'I'm sorry to say it *is*,' was her quiet reply.
'My pot of dreams never turns out the way
my recipe requires. To flatter me is useless.
I cannot help. Only Lady Alpenrose
may, and she's not been seen for over a year.
I *think* I know why but that alone won't find her.'

'Surely you can do so! If you're kind enough
to try, choose any cow, sheep or goat you like…'
'Wait and listen,' she answered calmly. 'What use
would your precious animals be to me?
Can I put them in my pot? Don't you realise
I only care for dreams. To me they are real,
not livestock nor any goods you may offer.'
The woodsman had no answer and turned away baffled
and convinced he'd lost his boy and girl for ever.

Well-wisher felt his despair and wanted
to say more if he would wait and hear her out.
'Don't lose patience!' Her voice was firm but kind.
Adam felt bound to obey and listen again.
'Sit by my fire and I'll ponder over
the pot I've simmered and stirred for a hundred years.
Perhaps it's time for me to discover a dream
that will tell you how to overcome the enchanter
and bring back your beloved Berwald and Clara.

For over an hour she stirred and sang to herself,
her tone and her face changing as good dreams surfaced
or bad ones were mixed away. Then suddenly
she said: 'Fængler can be weakened and defeated.
Someone must make the rose-hearted wish
despite their feelings. Your heart's too laden with dreams
of power for this. If only Lady Alpenrose
were not lost! She'd make all the difference to you.
I wonder how and why she's slipped beyond my knowledge.'

XIV

GENTIAN

*Flower guardians took bodily form to nurture families
of plants from new leafing till petals fell and seeds took passage.
Now few return each year to remote and hilly regions,
watching over spring growth and giving care in many guises.
So most herbs and shrubs thrive or wither without help
from their far-sighted keepers who once covered all countries.
Humans are lucky to see these lively, little-known beings,
yet they alone first spread forest speech among flowers
who often make their music to move our minds for the better.*

-◆-

'But not beyond mine!' said a playful voice
in forest speech from the hut door. They saw
nothing, until a small figure showed herself,
dressed entirely in deep blue, and radiant with joy
at being able to sing, dance and chatter, all
in quick succession, so you wondered which was which.
Her family had only a brief season of flowering,
and this kept her endlessly busy and cheerful.
She bowed on seeing the Wellwisher's visitor,
skipped across the floor and sat gracefully
on the edge of the frothing dream pot,
untouched by its fierce heat and fumes.
'What lovely dreams you have in there!
And, Mother Wellwisher, I notice those
tinted with rose starting to come true.'
'New ones!' said the sifter of dreams. 'They took
more stirring than usual. They become
true because good intentions begin them.'

'I saw some bad dreams, too,' said Gentian.
'This can't be helped,' said Wellwisher. 'Bad wishes
lead to dark, disturbing dreams. Perhaps you
can help me adjust them.' *'No, it's beyond me.'*
For a moment Gentian seemed less lively
and her words sounded unusually serious:
'People will keep wishing black or yellow.
Boys and grown men who should know better
are the worst. Nothing ever changes
till rose-hearted wishes rule their lives.'
She turned to look at Adam who was learning
forest talk again. Her words troubled him.
'Please explain black and yellow wishes,' he asked.
'Lady Alpenrose will show you.
Make it your first purpose to find her.'
'This talk is like a fox chasing its tail.
My main purpose is to find my two children.'
He stood up, took his stick, and made for the door.

'Be patient, Adam !' Wellwisher warned him again.
'Lose your temper and you'll lose your loved ones.'
'But you are so slow,' grumbled the forester.
'Like Time!' laughed the old dreamer. 'My long
life has taught me how to follow his slow pace.
He always arrives in the end. Now here's a dream
I've been waiting for. An old one that's surfaced
from deep in the pot. Taste it, Gentian!'
The flower guardian dipped her finger in the spoon
and tried a trace of it. *'That's calming and truthful,'*
she almost sang. *'I see how Adam may rescue*
his children, though he'll need to listen and learn.'
'I'll do what is required,' said Adam quietly.
'Rest here till night turns grey
but be on your way before dawn,
for when its first beam begins to slant
across the woods you'll see the Bright Beetle...'
Gentian had resumed her easy, tuneful tone.

'She'll creep from under a stone where she rests
and make her long journey to Fængler's forest,
taking a way only known by her,
one she can't reveal or talk about.
A spell the evil master's cast on her
will not be lifted till she gives a stranger
his chance to make the rose-hearted wish.
Fængler can't confine her to his realms
for he fears the force of her smiling spirit.
No one smiles or laughs where he rules
except his crazy spy-tower guards.'
'What will my Clara do?' exclaimed the woodsman.
'She laughs and sings from dawn to dusk.'
'Sorry as I feel, I cannot answer,' said Gentian.
'I've delayed too long. I must attend
to my flowers who need me most
before sundown.' So she sang her way downhill
and even Wellwisher's hut felt dull and empty.

Since greeting the wise dreamer at sunrise
Adam felt he'd lost track of time. Why had Gentian
suggested that evening was well on its way?
'Her visits surprise me,' said Wellwisher. 'I miss
that melodious voice and cheerful care for all
her charges. Now for a simple meal, then
you must rest thoroughly before the fire.
Tomorrow's journey will be longer and more eventful
than your trek up here. I'll wake you in time.'

'How can I pay you for your kind help?'
asked her guest. For answer she stood up and looked
into her pot, appearing taller and stronger
than Adam could ever have imagined her to be.
'Pay me! How can a Wellwisher be paid?'
she asked in a puzzled, offended voice. 'Suppose
I took your hard-earned money. I couldn't use it.
I only care for dreams. Perhaps when you return
you'll bring me one started by rose-hearted wishes.'

This did not lift his spirits. 'I can tell
your mind's on the wish-making chain,' she said.
'The thought of it weighs on you. But whoever
takes it from Fængler must bear in mind
its ancient purpose: to help those most in need.
Remember *that* or worse misfortunes may follow.
The wily old manipulator can be weakened
but only by the presence of rose-hearted wishes.
Anger or blows fuel the fire that consumes him.

'That wish again and again,' said Adam. 'Shrouded
in mystery as ever. I can't make it
and I doubt if you or anyone knows how.'
'Each of us finds a way,' she said. 'It can't be taught.
I wish you good night.' Soon he fell asleep
and dreamed he was pacing through a forest filled
with strange light that made him see and understand
more than when he was a child, and to his joy
he awoke and found none of this gift was lost.

XV

BRIGHT BEETLE

*Alpenrose would never turn away from any flower
still trying to make a meagre living on the margins
of Fængler's lands. He found her helping them to flourish
and took a long-awaited chance to change this cheerful Guardian
to a lowly creature locked in the limits of a spell.
As a young man who yearned for wisdom, he yielded
to her kindly advice till she cut too close to his pride.
She knew how misplaced love led him to live on anger.
For that she was punished. Not for protecting her plants.*

-◆-

When stars began to fade and a first
shaft of light would shoot down from the rocks
above the forest, Wellwisher left her pot
and woke Adam from the dream she'd provided
to help him learn again the woodland tongue he'd once
shared with all the plants and creatures of his valley.
He was soon ready to take this unlikely
chance, grabbed his stick and stuck his axe into
a broad belt. His kind adviser eyed the axe,
doubting its use in the day ahead of him,
while he was thinking it a foolish quest to follow
a beetle and ask its advice. Dawn was often
Adam's time for cool judgments, but the delight
of his dream with its sound of forest talk
made him set aside his impulse to break into
Fængler's haunts and threaten him with punishment.
'Look!' exclaimed Wellwisher. 'Any moment
light will leap from the mountain. Be ready!'

Behind snow-topped crags above the tips of pines
still standing in dark ranks, Adam saw
a rosy glow and then a beam that darted through
the trees and lit up a heap of splintered rock.
At once there emerged on swift, delicate legs
a tiny creature with a luminous green back.
It was the Bright Beetle setting out, as Gentian
predicted, her purpose fixed on a long journey.
'Hurry! She may spread her wings and leave you behind,'
warned the dreamer. 'If anyone tries to talk
don't stop. Keep her constantly in sight.
Giving her the chance to help may well
bless you both in unexpected ways.'
'Even so it's a slim chance,' said Adam,
still reluctant to rely on an insect.
'Best outcomes have small beginnings,' was all
the seer said before returning to her dreams.
And the beetle ran on regardless of who followed.

Always heading south she dropped down ravines cut
into the mountains by rapid streams, leapt from
stone to stone over torrents and scaled the far side
without a pause, to run across high summer
pastures grazed by cattle Adam did not recognise.
To keep her bearings she often took tortuous paths
only fit for goats or sheep. The forester followed,
admiring her pluck and skill, though he feared
for his life as she crossed treacherous shelves
of sloping rock where *he* would never have ventured.
He couldn't tell if she was aware of her companion,
yet why did she only spread her wings and fly
when the steepest ground checked her urgent pace?
And so they travelled into the June afternoon,
Adam only taking quick drinks from streams,
and descended to the eastern pass where wolves
howling at sunset had frightened his children into
finding shelter by the light of the prying moon.

They passed the crag where Woolly Edelweiss
had lectured Berwald and Clara. He expected attention
and liked to know everyone's business. 'What's the hurry?'
he squeaked. Adam recalled Wellwisher's words,
kept his eye on the Beetle and said nothing.
The Red Eagle had not missed Adam's rapid
scramble across his wide hunting domain and hoped
to find out its purpose. Pretending to be perched
by chance on a rock beside the path, he screamed:
'Your're heading in entirely the wrong direction.'
Adam's answer was to brandish his axe that flashed
with such sudden anger it quite unnerved
the conceited hawk who took off none the wiser.
Later they approached Fængler's spy tower
with its outstretched wings of rocky walls.
Clipetty and Clopitty were aware
but went unchallenged. The Beetle had her own
secret access to the master's shadowy hideouts.

To her follower's relief the Beetle at last stopped
for a rest, though she then appeared to vanish.
Exhausted he threw himself down on a bank
of stiff upland grass and felt the edge of his axe
only to hear a gentle voice beside his ear.
The Beetle had alighted on a ledge above him.
'That may be a sturdy axe,' she said.
*'But you don't know the kind of power Fœngler
wields, and he won't give up its chained source
without trying every devious means he knows.'*
Such serious, well-phrased warnings from a beetle
amused Adam. 'I've always wanted to face him,'
he said. 'I look forward to the chance you've kindly
led me to take. Surely I have the strength
to crush that old villain. A nanny goat
could easily butt him off his feet!'
His guide gave a sigh and smiled to herself,
hard as this may be to imagine.

'Travellers should rest as light fails,'
she said. *'We're tired after our many miles.
We will enter Fœngler's woods after
sunrise tomorrow. Time to tell a tale
I think you should hear. But refresh
yourself with a long sleep before
you say even a single word about it.
What you hear will, without your knowing,
return vividly in several dreams.'*
'As you wish,' said Adam politely.
'But why can't we press on soon and reach
my children before they suffer worse torments?'
'The enchanter is weakest at dawn,'
said the Beetle. *'And there's much
you have to learn before we set foot
in the shadowy, joyless lands he controls.
You must go at my pace. Besides, I know
the password to make the guard admit us.'*

XVI

FÆNGLER

{{The tale Bright Beetle told to Adam}}

*The evil master began as a bronze-bearded craftsman
eager to refine his skills. But his sharp mind and subtle soul
were concealed in a coarse face and crooked figure.
They called him 'Altfänger' as he aged into cunning ways,
took to lurking in Trocktal and turned night-time thief.
'The Old Catcher' for one who filched from others,
a mean hoarder who hurt men happy with their lot,
though figures never seen are known by many names.
'Fængler' or 'Fangless' were often used to fit the felon.*

Gerard was the birth name given to Fængler.
And soon after his father died of a fever,
leaving a mother to manage her only child,
who grew so used to having his way
few could guide him against his will.
But he studied hard and learnt to solve
many a problem that baffled older men.
Early apprenticed in the art of carving wood
his delicate work attracted many dealers.

From the age of ten he grew no taller
though he broadened and shambled like a bear.
Loathing how he looked people laughed
or tried to hide from him. And he hid from them,
in his work place or walking alone at night.
For fools he had no time and told them so,
making enemies of many who admired him.
Wild creatures and plants were his company
until they pointed out the poison in his soul.

But there was one person he wished to please,
a lady who'd long had his loyal service,
daughter to a rich count who took rent
from all who worked the land of his wide valley.
The family lived in a five-towered castle
set in terraced gardens on a rocky slope.
Fængler still sees it from his spy tower.
The count invited all kinds of clever men
to bring cheer to his bored and lonely child.

Miriam, *the longed-for*, was born with the loss
of her mother who'd mourned for many children.
The girl favoured Gerard when she felt inclined,
then scorned him to see the way he squirmed.
Once she plucked a rose and playfully
presented it with a pertly winning smile.
A joke to her became his close-kept joy.
If only his wealth and wisdom could outweigh
his looks, she might be moved to marry him.

He dreamed of a gift to delight her,
a castle he'd construct from mother of pearl.
He'd show her his sketches and seek her advice.
But then he heard of her heart's utmost desire,
to wield the power of the ancient Wishing Chain
whose making consumed so many years and minds.
He forgot his plans and found his way to Wellwisher
who surely knew the secret of its whereabouts.
He respected what her dreams revealed to him.

She understood and guided Gerard without
making him suffer more self doubt.
From her pot of dreams she picked the one
he needed, though he never grasped the true
sense of what she found for him. Fond hopes
of riches and power turn dreams the wrong colour.
The necklace, he learnt, had been hidden or lost,
buried for countless years in slime below a pool
and fountain which somehow seemed familiar.

Was it by the maze where Miriam and her maids
sat to shelter from sun or sharp winds?
The still edge gave her a glass to gaze at
while her attendants praised those perfect looks,
flattery she never failed to believe.
Gerard could come or go as he pleased,
so he'd wait for this train of ladies to wander
down the terraces, then pass a tough test
of devotion by diving for what she most desired.

One fine morning he followed at a distance
and saw his lady sitting in the shade beside
the pool, laughing with her lively company.
In glistening ivory gown she outshone the gathering.
He waved from the far side of the water,
bowed like a courtier and blew her a kiss.
(A clown cutting into their conversation!)
Intent on his exploit he imagined
their mockery meant encouragement.

She'd heard how a handsome nobleman asked
her father for her hand but he'd flatly refused:
the man was poor and she must marry into wealth.
Oh to find that necklace and wish him a fortune!
She'd no idea that Gerard intended to find it,
and when he dived in with a muddy splash,
hoping everyone would admire his feat,
they supposed he must have lost his senses
or was it his latest ploy to make them laugh?

'When I am married he can entertain me
as court fool,' said Miriam . But this was no fool
groping in the slimy depths of a green pool,
fouling its waters till he thought he felt a wire
loop round his wrist, and with a wrench released
the clogged chain, surfaced with a choked cry,
leapt up in the water and lurched towards the bank.
'Look what I've brought for my bride to be!
Wear it on your swan-white neck and make your wishes!

Let me kiss you to confirm my promise.'
'Kiss Master Gerard with his pock-marked face,
shaggy red beard, and body all out of shape!
I'd rather go and kiss one of my father's goats.
Marry you! Should I laugh or scream in horror?'
Looking at his matted hair and mud-stained skin
she said: 'You've betrayed yourself. Be off for good!'
Her maids' harsh laughter hit rocky parapets,
flapped against plane trees and fluttered through pine groves.

He stood there dripping and dejected, looked down
into the now still, clear water and saw
his discoloured face and crooked little figure.
How ugly he was! What countess could wed him?
Why not throw this necklace back? It was the noose
that strangled his hope of securing a lady's favour.
Let someone else wallow after it
and try their luck with the useless trinket.
How could he prize what had failed to please?

Then he heard Miriam tittering among her maids
as they scuttled back to the castle, and her scorn
burnt into him and left a bitter taste.
Her mocking contempt closed his heart to love, laughter
and acts of kindness. Why not keep the chain
and use it to make everyone pay for all
he had suffered? *(Good fortune will smile on no one*
if I can help it. To be hated will be
my success. They'll see who's master.)

XVII

ALPENROSE

*A long, narrow stretch of green, life-giving land
ran between Fængler's woods and the foothills of Fürst,
jagged peaks without path or pass for man or beast.
This margin divided mountain from man-made forest
thanks to the old trickster who thought himself under threat
even from a long-lost legend telling how these crags unleashed
phantom invaders to avenge ancient wrongs on all in their path.
But they feared bright spirits formed in fertile places,
a barrier like a broad river that drove them back.*

NOTE
The cluster of sharp pinnacles some called **Fürst** might have once been *Der Fürst der Finsternis* (The Prince of Darkness) and the old legend was probably linked to that name.

Before he fell asleep Adam had not missed
a word of the tale. It felt like the next
minute when her voice woke him. *'Make haste!*
we must set out before the sun's first
rays touch those slopes to our west!'
Crawling from under bushy pines which had covered
his deep sleep, he shook yesterday's many
weary miles from his stiffened back and legs.
A dim light glowed in the east above
the menacing mass of Fængler's woods.
Time to talk to the beetle about her tale
and measure how it had changed his feelings.
'Now I no longer hate the old deceiver.
I pity his dark and lonely life. I'll make him
return my children but I care no more about
the necklace of stones or what I may wish.
If that lost soul leaves us all in peace,
we'll be glad to live without wealth or power.'

The Beetle made no reply but Adam heard
a sharp crack rip through the air as if
someone had fired a gun at close range.
The insect's brilliant green mantle was splitting apart
and before Adam's eyes she vanished. From her coat
emerged the loveliest womanly form he'd ever seen.
Her golden hair reminded him of ripe corn
and he was amazed at how her rose-coloured gown
seemed to be made of layer upon layer of petals.

Taking the woodsman's right hand in both of hers,
to his confusion she thanked him for his help.
'My tale has moved you to make the rose-hearted wish
and that has freed me from Fœngler's spell.
You have released the Guardian known to many
as Alpenrose, who can now resume her work.'
Adam leapt up, removed his frayed hat,
and bowed low to this radiant presence who must
have taken shape from the sun's first rays.

She laughed at his surprise and ran with joy
among her flowering plants who added a rosier glint
to her gown. *'We must be on our way,'* she said.
*'Light's growing fast and our evil host
waits in his cave. The solemn sentinel
will be so taken aback when he sees me
as I am, he'll let us in to the dense wood.'*
Following her between foothills and forest
Adam thought trees and shrubs glowed with rosy light.

'How did you ever turn into a beetle?'
asked Adam. *'That can't be told simply,'* she said.
*'I tried to stop the wily thief carrying children
away from valleys below his fenced-off haunts.
When they wandered away from their homes I'd wrap
them in rose colour to keep the cold at bay,
an aura that confused and frightened Fœngler,
who also hated me for crossing his borders to keep
my plants alive. Worse, when he consulted me
about his wishes and worries, I never pleased him.
One spring day a bitter easterly wind
made me anxious about my plants and I forgot
to be happy. Catching me off guard he seized
his chance to turn me into a black beetle,
but keeping myself cheerful and useful
soon changed my coat to glossy green.
Only the rose-hearted wish could reverse the spell.
Years may pass before someone makes it fully.'*

The distance between the slopes to the west
and Fœngler's thick pine forest to the east
narrowed, so they could see the tall palisade
that fenced them out. This looked so forbidding
Adam felt doubly impatient to reach his children.
Then Alpenrose suddenly vanished
under thorn bushes, led him over a dyke
and through a rocky gully to a spiked gate,
a secret entrance still far from the caves.

'The solemn guard sits here if he's disgraced
for any reason his master chooses to pick on.
He's there! Watch him when he sees me!'
This down-hearted slave who'd watched over
Berwald and Clara in Dead Wood and hid
when Fængler approached, still trembled from
his master's rage as he peeped through the gate
he hated guarding. The tyrant's red, scowling face
filled his mirror and kept him at his post.

Few strangers found their way into the confined
rock cavern that concealed this small gate.
That two were now approaching terrified the guard.
To make it worse a rosy light surrounded
the visitors, a colour that inspired fear
among everyone Fængler's gloom had subdued.
'There's nothing to be afraid of,' said Alpenrose gently.
'But…but…' he stammered. *'No Buts!'* she said.
'Except one: you will learn to laugh again!'
And she kissed his anxious face through the bars.
He dropped his mirror and trembled even more,
then a trace of merriment twinkled in his eyes.
For years he could not number he'd wanted to smile
but now it felt as easy and natural as breathing.
*'The password **Black Wish** has been thrown away,'*
said Alpenrose. *'It's now **Rose-hearted Wish**,*
and soon there'll be no gates to guard or chain up.
It's a password for all, even the master!'

'Come in, and welcome!' said the relieved guard,
unlocking the hated frame of iron spikes
for the last time, he hoped. The Guardian
found the mirror and handed it to Adam.
He saw a desolate marsh surrounded by
steep, rocky slopes. Cows and goats picked
their way over it, trying to graze.
They were so thin and unkempt he only
knew which were his by their bells and collars.

Nearby Clara sat on a grey boulder,
her dress torn and stained from the long fall
when she and Berwald were pitched into the luckless dale.
She could not cry, which made her more wretched.
Berwald was doing his best to look for
something to eat and a source of fresh water.
His eyes alone told a tale of hunger and fear.
Adding to their prisoner's diet devoured
his thoughts. The necklace might never have been there.

'Show me how to reach my children!' shouted Adam,
ready to force march the frightened sentinel.
'The only route, I'm afraid, is through
Fængler's cave and passage ways,' was the reply.
The thought of that made the guard feel hopeless
but he continued. 'Alpenrose can guide you,
forester, only let me warn you:
entering the cave is easier than finding an exit.'
For some reason this reminded him how
he had learnt to smile and he did so for practice.
It gave him courage and he now hoped
something would surprise him into laughing.
Meanwhile, Adam took the lead, and soon
they were striding down the long avenue
that led from the fortress to the master's cave.
Here Clara's secret wish had terrified him.
A self-important guard at the cave mouth
seemed unable to speak or hold them back.

This weakness came from within the cave.
Sensing a presence he was powerless to ward off
Fængler sat huddled in a corner clutching
his coat round him to hide the now useless chain.
His fire made acrid smoke to blind and choke intruders;
but Adam plunged in, tripping over a helpless sentry.
The forester's fury gave the deceiver sudden strength
to defeat his enemy with the blackest of wishes,
until he saw Alpenrose and shivered in dismay.

Where could he hide in the blaze of rose light
that filled the vault? How had she broken free
from his spell? Her rescuer now stood
face to face with the one who'd long tormented
so many happy and harmless valley people,
the heartless bully who'd stolen and starved children,
driven off cattle and filched goods to hurt his neighbours.
He grabbed a handful of rope-strong beard
and dragged the villain out of his hiding place.

'Fængler, once called Gerard, you've plundered and pilfered
for more than a hundred years. Now you've taken
my children and I demand them back.' Adam's captive
cursed and yelled, twisting and turning to break free.
'Don't blame me. They came here and took their chance.'
'Like my cattle and goats!' said Adam, dragging him
out into the wood towards a stout pine.
Now you'll get what you've long deserved;
even the rose-hearted wish can't save you.'

XVIII

NECKLACE

Despised by Miriam, Fængler was driven to despair,
loathed and stamped out laughter, love and kindness.
However cruel his spells captives were not maimed or killed
but made to suffer that same dark state of mind.
No magic chain will change one who cheats himself.
To him its stones meant little, nor did he learn to link their powers.
The necklace lost its soul like its hopeless owner
who was drawn to juggle only with red jasper and black jet,
making wrongful wishes lead to worse, with no way out.

Adam found a stake and coiled the prisoner's beard
round and round it, drew his axe and hewed a cleft
in the trunk of a carefully chosen pine.
He lifted the weak old trickster on to a branch
below the notch and thrust in the rough stake
wrapped tightly with a length of tangled beard.
'Now, Fængler, move and you'll hurt yourself
more than you can bear. You can't touch the ground
and you'll just hang helplessly by your beard.
Sit still and you'll feel nothing except shame
for your miserable life, unless that's beyond you.'
'I've no strength or wish to move,' was the answer.
'It's more than you deserve to have the choice', said Adam.
'I ought to shake you. Once for my cows and goats.
Twice for Alpenrose. Three times for my children.
Three more for making their mother suffer so much.
When I've found my children, I'll be back to do so.'
He squealed like a trapped rat: *'If you'd free me...!'*

'Learn what your victims have felt,' replied Adam,
who picked up his axe and strode away, while Alpenrose
felt pity, which only made the captive weaker.
Though as she followed Adam back into the cave,
while Fængler screamed out offers of flocks and precious gifts,
she was careful not to let her feelings take control.
Then it suddenly struck Adam that in his concern
to confront the villain with his evil ways,
find his children and bring comfort to Maria,
he'd forgotten the necklace. But this followed
from the selfless wish that had released the Guardian.
Fængler had also tucked the chain out of sight.
While his loved ones were lost and suffering
Adam did not care where it was, or notice
how a crowd seethed round the cave mouth.
Enslaved spirits had emerged. The once solemn guard
stood among them smiling, while they mocked the captive
who looked as if he were caught in one of his spells.

Closely followed and guided by Alpenrose
dispersing the dark with rosy dawn, Adam rushed
along the confusing labyrinth of passages
behind Fængler's cave. The great door made of
tree trunks stood open, and perched on the gate
into Dead Wood the robin welcomed them
with his most jubilant song, the first
joyful sound to fill that bleak spot for more
than a century. Adam smiled his thanks
for he understood the bird's celebration,
then he plunged down the rough track that dropped
into Luckless Dale. Long before he was down
among the scrub and marshes the children saw him
and found new strength to scramble, run and climb
towards him. Not for a moment did Clara
feel too old to be lifted up and held
in her father's strong arms or to let her tears
of relief show she was content to be there.

Berwald kept his feelings close. He'd begun
to realise his wishes had brought on worse
trouble once they'd crossed Fængler's borders.
Knowing how he felt the Guardian touched his shoulder
to show her sympathy. He looked up into
her clear blue eyes and knew this adventure
would change his wishes for the better.
He didn't know how. Perhaps she made him feel
mistakes are stepping stones, not stumbling blocks.

Adam called away his cows, sheep and goats
and those from other farms soon followed, but first
to come was Ladybrown, the children's comforter.
The winding passages would fill them with fear and panic
so the Guardian summoned some woodland spirits
to open a disused track between Dead Wood
and the massive rocks above the old mines.
Guided out and on towards the eastern pass
they'd graze well before being herded home.

As they walked underground, back towards
the cave where the master's fire still smouldered,
Clara clung closely to her father. He headed
straight for the pine to which he'd fastened
the old thief, still wriggling in fear and anger.
Begging Adam for freedom, he promised him
rich rewards. The father could only think about
how his children had been treated. Clara at once
felt sorry for the captive and forgot his cruelty.
She saw how feeble and fragile he really was,
and all the more pitiful for being so ugly.
She thought of his lonely, smoke-filled cave,
where he sat and brooded over ways to harm
those who shunned and hated him. Even his servants
only obeyed out of fear, and longed for release.
Words she tried to find for this were lost in tears.
Joy or sorrow flowed freely now Fængler's bitter
soul no longer spread its gloom over the land.

Adam thought she was homesick and promised
she'd soon be back with Mother and Baby. 'Something else
troubles me,' she said, looking at the helpless, trapped
old man. He stopped struggling and looked back.
Then his face seemed to change. Was it the first
trace of a shy, twisted little smile in one
corner of his mouth ? Perhaps for a moment
Clara looked like the Miriam he loved and served
before her scorn turned him against delight and pleasure.

Reaching inside his cracked leather coat he seemed
to pull out and over his head a length of old rope.
'Take it, Clara,' he said wearily. 'It weighs
me down. My wishing has come to an end.
You deserve the necklace. Given as a gift
it's harmless, and only good wishes will prevail.'
As he spoke the chain lost its tarnish,
every stone and link blazed with new life,
and it looked smaller and lighter in his hand.

'Thank you for this kindness,' said Clara, running
without fear to receive the precious gift.
' I'll give it to father. He'll know how and when
to use it for the best. I'm not wise enough.'
In Adam's broad, weathered palm it looked
flimsy and out of place. He thanked her gently
and put it in a safe pocket, though he wondered
whether it could make changes for the better
now he'd rescued his beloved children and flocks.

'Let's set the old man free before we go,'
said Clara. 'He's been kind at last, and he's weak.
You're sorry for him, too, aren't you Berwald?'
He hesitated at first, then spoke firmly:
'Yes, I am now. Let's free him.
My plans and wishes increased his evil powers.
Now he can't hurt people or beasts.'
Adam looked hard at the helpless figure,
and at his boy and girl. He remembered
the tale of Gerard's hopeless quest to please Miriam,
followed by a fruitless life without love.
'You're right,' he admitted. 'Without the chain
he can harm no one. He won't wander far
from his forest ever again.' He unwound
the stake, smoothed out the tangled beard,
and lifted down a limp, trembling body
that could hardly stand. Adam steadied him
and offered his own stick as a support.

Fængler could hardly believe this good will.
Looking only at Clara he gave her thanks
without words, took Adam's stick and limped away
into the depths of the forest he'd planned and planted.
No rumours of his whereabouts ever came
to the valleys. His wishes mattered no more.
This was not the success Adam or Berwald
had long looked forward to, but like Clara
they were now intent on the quickest way home.

It was hard to believe the sun would go down
on what was only the fourth day of their
long, tiring adventures. They hurried along
the gloomy forest avenue, through the open gates
and unattended vaults of the fortress,
lately abandoned by Clipetty and Cloppity,
then took the track to the great pass.
Edelweiss was eager for detailed news. They waved,
leaving him to squeak with offended pride.

Circling high to search for prey, Red Eagle
spotted Adam hand in hand with his children.
Like his forbears he sniffed out a victory,
so he perched near the path to have a part
in the triumph. But he croaked congratulations
to no effect. His advice had deceived Berwald,
who felt ashamed, and did all he could
to keep the others talking in case the pompous hawk
tried to remind him of his boastful behaviour.

Then they crossed a patch of lingering snow
where Soldanella and her sisters welcomed them
with a modest concert of purple, tinkling bells.
And as they came down the steep, twisting path
from the pass to the ford over Mittelbach,
many clusters of Gentians danced, even without
a mountain breeze, celebrating their return
with ancient songs in the forest tongue.
Their favourite Clara understood all they sang.

Maria stood by the chalet with baby in her arms.
The sight they'd longed for. She gave him to Adam
so the lost ones could fall into her arms
and forget they'd ever left home. As they all
embraced, many nearby pines seemed to glow
with rose-coloured lights, while Alpenrose sang
a happy melody that echoed through the woods,
joyfully answered by cows and goats with their bells.
Perhaps the best wishes do come true.

LaVergne, TN USA
10 September 2010
196630LV00005B